Alfred Lee

Memoir of Benjamin Lee

Addressed to his grandchildren by his son Alfred Lee

Alfred Lee

Memoir of Benjamin Lee
Addressed to his grandchildren by his son Alfred Lee

ISBN/EAN: 9783337219826

Printed in Europe, USA, Canada, Australia, Japan

Cover: Foto ©Raphael Reischuk / pixelio.de

More available books at **www.hansebooks.com**

MEMOIR
OF
Benjamin Lee.

Addressed to his grand-children
by his
SON
Alfred Lee

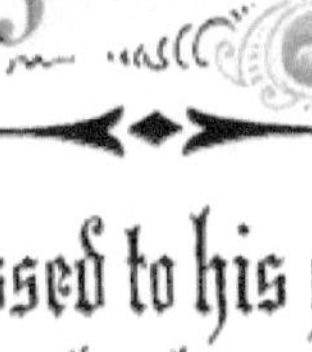

"Justum ac tenacem propositi virum."

Benjamin Lee

Benjamin Lee the subject of this Memoir, was born in Taunton, Somersetshire, England, February 26th, 1765. My impression is that his father's name was Thomas. He at one time carried on the manufacture of cloth upon a somewhat extensive scale, but must have suffered from reverses in business. In his religious views he was a dissenter, and so I think was his father before him. All that I ever heard of the latter was an anecdote related by my father. He was a man of very methodical habits and particularly regular and punctual in attendance at his place of worship. One Saturday night he retired to rest with the impression strong upon his mind that he must be up betimes for the services of the Sabbath. He rose in his sleep, dressed himself, and was awakened at the church door by the clock striking the midnight hour.

My grandfather was married twice. His second wife, my grandmother, was Mary Pitt, one of the family which gave two eminent statesmen to Great Britain. Mr. John Pitt Letche, my father's nephew, says in a letter to my mother, written in

1845. "The mother of your husband was a Pitt. The head of the family about a century ago was a country gentleman of good estate, residing on his ancient family mansion, at Charlton-Somerton, Somersetshire. His son, through his great talents, became Earl of Chatham, whose son was the celebrated William Pitt, the Premier Minister of England. The family and title are now extinct. My honored grandmother was a favorite with the family."

The affection of her son Benjamin for his mother was very strong, and he was able to provide for her comfort in her widowhood and old age. She was an attached member of the Church of England, and from her were derived my father's predilections for the Episcopal Church, which have proved, under the guidance of divine Providence, the means of bringing all his descendants within that fold.

There were two sets of children. Those of the first wife, so far as my knowledge extends, were Thomas, Joseph, and John, possibly one or more daughters. Of the second wife, Mrs. Letche and your grandfather were children. Respecting two daughters, one who was married to Mr. Coffin Jones, of Boston, and another married to Dr. Marshall Spring, of Watertown, near Boston, I am uncertain.

Thomas, the eldest son, owing, I presume, to his father's reverses, came to America, and entered into mercantile business in Boston, a step which had important influence upon the family history. He had a thorough business training, having taken an active part in his father's affairs. He entered into partnership with Mr. Coffin Jones, above mentioned, and the firm were among the leading merchants of Boston for a number of years prior to the American Revolution. Thomas Lee accumulated a fortune which would be considered handsome at the present day, and at that period was proportionately much larger. At the breaking out of the war, which put a stop to commercial business, he withdrew from Boston, and spent some time in Norwich and Pomfret, in Connecticut. In the latter place he was long remembered. He was fond of hunting, and scoured the country upon trained English hunters, astonishing the people by leaping gates and fences in the chase. I am inclined to think that during the struggle with England his sympathies were with the colonies, but he held himself aloof from political affairs. One result of the war was the fixing of his future residence in what was then the pleasant village of Cambridge, a place dear to me as my birthplace and early home, and afterwards the scene of my education.

The State of Massachusetts took possession of some vessels belonging to his firm, and fitted them out as cruisers. In compensation, Mr. Lee received the estate in Cambridge, on which he resided during the remainder of his life. It had belonged to Sewell, Attorney-General under the Crown, who fled to Nova Scotia. His property was confiscated as that of a Royalist and Refugee.

The house situated about half a mile from the University, on the road leading to what is now known as Mount Auburn, as well as the adjoining residence of the poet Longfellow, has an historic interest. It was in early times known as the Lechmere House, its neighbor being the Vassall House. The poet, in one of his beautiful little pieces, refers to it as "the old house among the lindens." I copy a notice which appeared in an article entitled "A Pilgrimage to the Cradle of American Liberty," by B. J. Lossing, published in Harper's Monthly Magazine, November, 1850.

"A few rods above the residence of Professor Longfellow is the house in which the Brunswick General, the Baron Riedesel, and his family were quartered during the stay of the captive army of Burgoyne in the vicinity of Boston. I was not aware, when I visited Cambridge, that the old mansion was still in existence; but, through the kindness of Mr. Longfellow, I am able to present the features of its southern front with a description. In style it is very much like that of Washington's headquarters (Longfellow's residence), and the general appearance of the grounds around is similar. It is shaded by noble linden-trees, and adorned with shrubbery, presenting to the eye all the attractions noticed by the Baroness Riedesel in her charming letters. Upon a window-pane on the north side of the house may be seen the undoubted autograph of that accomplished woman, inscribed with a diamond point."

The Baroness writes thus respecting her residence: "We were then transferred to Cambridge, where we were lodged in one of the best houses of the place, which belonged to Royalists. Seven families, who were connected by relationship, or lived in great intimacy, had here farms, gardens, and splendid mansions, and, not far off, orchards, and the buildings were at least a quarter of a mile distant from each other. The owners had been in the habit of assembling every afternoon in one or another of these houses, and of diverting themselves with music or dancing, and lived in affluence, in good humor and without care, until this unfortunate war at once dispersed them, and transformed all their houses into solitary abodes, except two, the proprietors of which were also soon obliged to make their escape." The Baroness here beguiled her captivity and celebrated her husband's birthday by entertaining the generals and officers of Burgoyne's army with a supper and illumination, at which "God save the King!" was sung with great enthusiasm.

In this pleasant mansion Mr. Thomas Lee spent the remainder of his days, enjoying in the style of a wealthy English gentleman his ample fortune. His dignified and affable manners, high standing, and free hospitality attracted to his house the best society of Boston and vicinity. His dwelling was handsomely furnished, and he had also a good library and philosophical apparatus. He had in his stables fine imported horses, and when on the occasion of some religious assemblage he visited Philadelphia, in company with President Willard of Harvard College, he took the President on with him in his coach and four. He was a member of the Congregational Church in Cambridge, of which the Rev. Abiel Holmes, D.D., father of Oliver Wendell Holmes, was pastor for many years. Of the sincerity of his piety he gave evidence by open-handed benevolence and an unspotted life. He was a benefactor of the College, and his name may be seen above one of the alcoves in the Library.

To the Cambridge House were attached about forty acres of land, extending to the borders of Fresh Pond. The garden and orchard were stocked with choice fruit, some kinds then growing freely, as the sweet-water grape and the peach, which cannot now be raised in the open air. Some of the fine linden-trees, above mentioned, were blown down before my astonished eyes by the September gale of 1815, and were afterwards replaced by my father, with the help of oxen and pulleys. The house is still standing, although much changed—in my opinion not for the better—

by what are called modern improvements. After the death of Mr. Thomas Lee's widow it was occupied by my father until about 1819, when it passed into the hands of Andrew Craigie, being part of the consideration for the lands purchased by my father of Mr. Craigie in Western New York.

Mr. Thomas Lee was married, in the city of Boston, by the Rev. Dr. Chauncey, to Miss Jane Miller, October 11, 1770. This marriage did not add to his happiness, his wife being a person of capricious disposition and unpleasant temper. He departed this life, at Cambridge, on Friday, May 25, 1797. His tomb, of elegant Italian marble, inclosed by an iron railing, is conspicuous in the old burial ground on Cambridge Common. I had the tomb placed in thorough repair in 1870, and would recommend, when any of the family are in Cambridge that they visit it and see that it does not fall into ruins. The remains of my brother Edmund were deposited there in 1836, and some of my father's children, who died in infancy, were also buried there.

The crayon portrait of Thomas Lee, now hanging in my library, supposed to be the work of Copley, presents an open, benignant countenance, corresponding well with what we know of his character. The resemblance is very discernible to some of his grand-nephews and nieces. This estimable man had no children. His property was left to his wife with the solemn charge, given to her on his death-bed, that from her it should go to his brother Benjamin. This promise was not sacred in her eyes. She lived until September 27, 1805.

Her eccentricities became more marked after her husband's death. She had a passion for hoarding, and large sums in gold were secreted by her in cellars and cupboards. She wandered about in the night, like a restless spirit, visiting her treasures; and her figure, clothed in a white robe, seen through the windows at late hours, suggested ghost stories. She was preyed upon by a set of parasites who were bent upon getting her fortune after her death, and obtained her signature to a will of the contents of which she knew but little. Elbridge Gerry, afterwards Vice-President, whose residence was about half a mile distant, visited her in her last illness, and, at her request, read to her the will she had executed. She emphatically declared, upon hearing it, that such was not her will. Mr. Gerry, I believe, represented to her the wrong done to my father, and to the wishes of her husband, and she had a lawyer immediately brought and made another will. After her funeral the persons engaged in the iniquitous scheme assembled, full of eager expectation, to listen to the reading of the important document. The scene of surprise, disappointment and rage, which ensued, was such as a Dickens would have delighted to describe. As it was, the property was greatly diminished by a very large number of legacies, and by extortionate charges of Executors and others,—but my brother Thomas was made the principal heir. As his guardian, my father took possession of the place. When Thomas arrived at the age of twenty-one, an arrangement, mutually beneficial, was made between himself and his father.

The prosperous condition of Thomas Lee attracted others of the family to this country, some of whom, by their unreasonable claims, occasioned him no little annoyance. His brother John had been educated for the Law, but became an ardent politician and a writer for the newspapers. He was a man of ability, but sadly intemperate, speedily squandering any money that came into his possession, and looking to his relatives for help in his difficulties. While in America he was a source of much vexation to his brother Thomas. The larger part of his life was spent in London. When my brother Thomas was in London, in 1820, John Lee found him out and presented himself, looking very poor and shabby and soliciting assistance. His death could not have been long after.

Joseph obtained a commission in the English Army, married and settled at Kingston, Jamaica. The only particular respecting him that I remember hearing, and it made quite an impression on my youthful mind, was that in a fit of anger, arising probably from some refusal of his brother to gratify his demands, he rode his horse up the steps of the house at Cambridge into the hall. While we were living at Cambridge, in the winter of 1818, his two daughters, Mary and Elizabeth, the first married and named Curtin, made us a visit and remained for a considerable time. Their father had been dead for some years and their mother was remarried. When I visited Kingston, in 1863, I inquired respecting the family, and ascertained that both my cousins were dead, and no representative remained.

Of my father's sisters I have little knowledge. Mrs. Letche remained in England and received for some years an allowance from him. Her son, John Pitt Letche, corresponded with my mother as late as 1845, and to his letters I am indebted for some interesting particulars. Major John Goldsworthy, who served for many years in India, was a relative and early friend of my father. I spent some days with him in December, 1830, and June, 1831, at his residence, Ackworth House, near Pontefract, Yorkshire, and saw at Taunton his sister, a maiden lady advanced in years, and a married daughter of the Major. I now come to your grandfather's personal history.

Benjamin Lee as a boy was noted for strength and activity, generosity and fearlessness. He was naturally impetuous and high spirited. For some small offence at school, in those days of rigid discipline, he was sentenced to a severe and disgraceful punishment. He rushed out of school. Some of the boys were sent to seize him and bring him back, but he distanced his pursuers by swimming a small river. I presume he did not return to bid them farewell that were in his house, but started at once for London. It would be interesting to know the particulars of his journey, but I do not think he ever spoke of it except to his wife. I have heard only a single incident. On his arrival in London he repaired to the counting house of an uncle after whom he was named, then a merchant in the city. The uncle received him rather coldly and handed him a guinea. The nephew indignantly threw the coin at his uncle's feet and departed. I suppose the fugitive must have had some experience of privation and sorrow in the great metropolis. The next that I know is his appointment as a midshipman in the Navy, and his being placed for instruction at a government school. I am not aware whether this appointment was procured by the agency of his brother Thomas, or by the influence of his mother's family. In 1783 he had advanced so far as to be placed in command of a battery of guns in the great naval battle between Admiral Rodney and Count de Grasse. This engagement was fought, April 12th, 1783, near the island of Guadaloupe, the fleets on each side consisting of over thirty line-of-battle ships. "The ships were so near each other that every shot told, and those of the French being full of men, a dreadful carnage ensued. The Formidable, Sir George Rodney's ship, fired no less than eighty broadsides, and every other ship in proportion, and the gallantry of the French was in no instance inferior to that of their opponents. About noon the British admiral broke through the enemy's line; and immediately throwing out signals for the van to tack the British got to windward and completed the general confusion of the French squadron. In this state the contest continued with unabated violence till the close of the day, when the French admiral's ship, the Ville de Paris, struck to Sir Samuel Hood in the Bartleur. Four other ships of the line were taken, one was sunk and one blew up in the action. Sir Samuel Hood pursued the flying squadron, and on the 19th, overtook and captured two of them in the Mona passage, the Jason and the Caton, with two frigates. Sir George Rodney immediately proceeded with the ships and prizes to Jamaica, and on his return to England was honored with an English, and Sir Samuel Hood with an Irish, peerage."*

There is every reason to believe that the gallantry and good conduct of Benjamin Lee in this action gained honorable distinction. He himself considered his prospects of rising to eminence in his profession as very promising, and has spoken of the comparative positions of Nelson, who was serving in the same ship, and himself as being in his favor. But such hopes were speedily blighted, and his career as an officer of the English navy was brought to an unexpected termination. The circumstances connected with this juncture in his life are quite remarkable and have found place in English historical works.†

*Smollett's History of England. †Croly's Life of George IV.

I have spoken of his native impetuosity of disposition. With this he had a vehement impatience of wrong and tyranny. At school he was the champion of weak boys against overbearing bullies. On a scrap of paper in his handwriting I find the following: "I entered on the world's great stage young, with a heart warm and generous, and whose agents, the eyes, moistened at every scene of misery and distress, while I burned with ardor to draw my sword and redress every grievance that wanton injustice could inflict." Giving way too readily and rashly to these feelings he was brought into imminent peril of his life, being sentenced to be shot by a Court-martial, and only saved through the interposition of Prince William Henry, Duke of Clarence, afterwards King William IV.

I quote a letter from his nephew, Mr. J. P. Letche, with extracts cut from the London newspapers, published soon after King William's death. As there are some things mentioned in one account and not in another, I copy them all.

Letter of Mr. Letche to my mother:

"I beg to inclose a paragraph which I cut out of *The Times* newspaper of June 21, 1837. You will perceive it relates to your nearest relation. The anecdote, as I have heard it, was to the effect that my uncle was tried by a Court-martial, and condemned, for challenging his superior officer for countermanding his humane order relative to prisoners on board his ship. The Prince went to the Admiral and told him he would not leave him until he had given him a pardon for his brother Lee. This was granted, and brother Lee immediately quitted the service. On leaving his ship to go ashore at Port Royal, the whole fleet manned the yards and gave him three cheers,—an honor never before or since paid to a young officer. A second challenge was sent, the parties met, and the Lieutenant was wounded."

FIRST ENCLOSURE.

"At the death of George IV., the Duke of Clarence ascended the throne, on the 26th of June, 1830.

"When the Prince was at Port Royal, in 1783, a midshipman named Lee was condemned to be shot for insubordination. The whole body of midshipmen was deeply affected at this sentence. In this emergency Prince William Henry came forward and drew up a petition, to which he was the first to affix his name, and got the rest of the midshipmen in port to follow his example. He then went himself to the Admiral with the petition, and begged his comrade's life with so much earnestness, that he succeeded in saving him."

SECOND ENCLOSURE.

"Whilst his Royal Highness's vessel formed a part of Lord Hood's squadron, a court-martial, of which his lordship was the president, was held upon Mr. Benjamin Lee, on a charge of disrespect to a superior officer, of which he was found guilty, and was in consequence sentenced to death. The whole body of midshipmen were deeply affected at the calamity which had thus befallen their comrade, but knew not how to set about endeavoring to obtain a mitigation of the sentence, they hesitating to apply to Admiral Rowley, the Commander-in-chief, and there being no time to refer to the Admiralty. Prince William Henry having learned this state of feeling, his Royal Highness, in a manner that reflected on him the highest honor, generously stepped forward, and drawing up a petition, was himself the first to sign it, the rest doing the same. His Royal Highness then carried the petition to Admiral Rowley, and begging the life of Mr. Lee in the most pressing and urgent manner, the request was granted, and he was reprieved."

THIRD ENCLOSURE.

"PORT ROYAL, April, 1783.

"The last time Lord Hood's fleet was here, a court-martial was held on Mr. Benjamin Lee, midshipman, for disrespect to his superior officer, at which Lord Hood sat as President. The determination of the court was fatal to the prisoner, and he was condemned to death. Deeply affected as the whole body of the midshipmen were at the dreadful sentence, they knew not how to obtain a mitigation of it. Since Mr. Lee was ordered to execution they had not time to make their appeal to the Admiralty, and despaired of success in a petition to Admiral Rowley. His Royal Highness generously stepped forth, drew up a petition to which he was the first to set his name, and solicited the rest of the midshipmen in port to follow his example. He then himself carried the petition to Admiral Rowley, and in the most pressing and earnest manner, begged the life of our unhappy brother, in which he succeeded. We all acknowledge our warmest thanks to our humane, our brave and worthy Prince, who has so nobly exerted himself in preserving the life of his brother sailor."

The last account was evidently written by one of the midshipmen of the fleet, soon after the occurrence. It is a cause for rejoicing that public sentiment and the feeling even of military and naval officers respecting duelling has so greatly changed of late years. Your grandfather's conduct in sending the challenge only shows that, at the age of eighteen, educated in the naval service, he shared in the then prevailing sentiment; while the moving cause was no personal pique or quarrel, but indignation at wrong and cruelty. How strongly the feelings of the officers and men were enlisted on his side, was shown by the unexampled demonstration of honor and regard paid to him at his leaving the vessel.

It appears by the history of the times that the advantages gained by the English in this great battle were counterbalanced by subsequent disasters. On the 26th of July, Admiral Graves sailed from Jamaica with seven ships of the line, including the Ville de Paris and some other of the prizes, the Pallas frigate and about one hundred sail of merchantmen. They encountered on the banks of Newfoundland one of the most dreadful storms ever known in that quarter. Only two of the line-of-battle ships escaped, some foundering with all their crews. Your grandfather's disappointment was great when a course of naval distinction opening so brightly was suddenly interrupted. It is well to remember that thousands of his fellow sailors found a watery grave a few weeks after the victory, and but for the supposed misfortune he might have been one of the number.

After leaving the English navy your grandfather must have sought, with little delay, his brother Thomas. I have heard him say that he was commander of a ship at the age of nineteen, and this must have been either a vessel belonging to the firm of Lee & Jones, or one provided for him by his brother's influence. From this time he was in most affectionate relations with Thomas until the latter's death. He followed the calling of ship captain in the merchant service, for most of his time from 1784 till his marriage in 1797, sailing from the ports of Boston and New York. He made voyages to France, to Cape Horn and the Southern Ocean, and several to China. He was one of the first to carry the American flag to the distant East. It was one of the delights of my childhood to sit upon his knee and listen to stories of adventure and peril; of fights with sea-lions in Terra del Fuego, of his counteracting in the straits of Sunda the treacherous designs of the Malays to seize his vessel and massacre the crew, by inviting the chiefs to dinner and then stationing a sailor with a drawn sword behind each of them—of exposure to pestilence at Batavia—of his battling against the cold and tempests of a most severe winter for weeks on our coast, until his provisions were almost spent, a winter in which only two ships, besides his own, gained the harbor of Boston, and of more than one narrow escape from wreck and destruction. One incident I recollect his telling to show the advantage of being able to speak the French language, an acquisition which he made by spending some months at Angoulême, in France. While in the island of Mauritius, a French fleet came in and laid an embargo upon all vessels in port. The detention threatened would have utterly ruined his voyage. He obtained access to the French admiral and represented to him the disastrous consequences that would ensue. The admiral after listening to him, answered, "Sir, you have found my weak point. I shall sail to-night at such an hour. Get ready, and follow closely in the wake of my ship." This was done. He left the port unchallenged, and when fairly out at sea, the admiral wished him "Bon voyage."

It will be apparent from the trusts confided to him at so early an age, that your grandfather was a thorough seaman, and he united two essential qualities in a remarkable degree—prudence and courage. He was eminently cautious, and never ran useless risks or neglected any proper precautions, while he was perfectly fearless and self-possessed in danger. As an instance of the first quality, I would mention that on one of his voyages home from China, in which dispatch was particularly important, he never left the deck, day or night, except to make changes in his clothing. An incident illustrative of the latter trait I remember hearing from him. Walking in the streets of Canton, he met a young Englishman hotly pursued by a crowd of Chinese. Allowing the young man to pass, he posted himself in the narrow street, extending a stout cane to the opposite wall so as to bar the way, and when the pursuers came up looked them sternly in the face. The Chinese paused, contemplated for a few moments the resolute stranger, and then quietly withdrew. The young man warmly thanked my father as the preserver of his life. A Chinaman had attempted to snatch his watch out of his hand. On his resisting, a crowd collected with threatening gestures and chased him when he attempted to escape. No doubt the young man would have been robbed and murdered, but the rabble were intimidated by the bold bearing of a single determined man, armed only with a walking stick.

I recall another incident illustrative of his self-possession. At a port in the East Indies he procured for one of his sailors, who was sick, the services of a surgeon of a French man-of-war. The surgeon sent in a very exorbitant bill, to the amount of which my father objected. While in a room at a public house, the surgeon and another officer entered, locked the door after them and took out

To all *Emperors*, *Kings*, ſovereign *Princes*, *States* and *Regents*, and to their reſpective Officers civil and military,---and to all others whom it may concern:

I GEORGE WASHINGTON, PRESIDENT

OF THE UNITED STATES OF AMERICA, do make known, That *Benjamin See* – Captain of the *Ship* – called the *Fair American* – of the Burthen of about *three hundred seventeen* Tons, is a Citizen of the ſaid United States; and that the ſaid *Ship* – which he commands, belongs to Citizens of the ſaid United States: And as I wiſh that the ſaid *Benjamin See* – may proſper in his lawful Affairs, I do requeſt of all the before mentioned, and of each of them ſeparately, where the ſaid *Benjamin See* – ſhall arrive with his Veſſel and Cargo, that they will be pleaſed to receive him with Kindneſs, and treat him in a becoming Manner; permitting him on the uſual Tolls and Expences in paſſing and repaſſing, to navigate, paſs and frequent their Ports, Paſſes and Territories, to the End that he may tranſact his Buſineſs where, and in what manner he ſhall judge proper; and whereby I ſhall conſider myſelf obliged

IN TESTIMONY whereof, I have cauſed the Seal of the United States to be affixed to theſe Preſents, and have hereunto ſet my Hand, at the City of *Philadelphia* the *twenty third* Day of *November* – in the Year of our Lord, One thouſand ſeven hundred and ninety *One*. —

G^o Washington

By the President

Th: Jefferson

the key, charged my father with insulting conduct, produced two swords, and insisted either upon immediate payment of the whole charge, or fighting on the spot. My father remonstrated against the proceeding, and the parties seated at a table entered into a warm altercation, during which the swords were deposited on the table. Suddenly my father extended his hand and grasped the swords. He then dictated his own terms to the two dismayed Frenchmen.

On one voyage his life was in imminent danger from a conspiracy formed on board to murder him and seize his vessel. The instigator of this plot was the first mate, a man of respectable connections, and whose superior position and education enabled him to exercise great influence over the minds of his illiterate accomplices. The ship which my father then commanded was "The Fair American," of which the sea-letter, or passport from the State Department, is still preserved in the possession of his grandson, Benjamin Lee. It bears date November 23, 1791, and bears the signature of George Washington, President, and of Thos. Jefferson, Secretary of State. The ship sailed from Boston for the East Indies, December 2, 1791. Things went on in the usual manner until January 26, 1792, when as my father was pacing the deck a sailor said to him in an under-tone: "Captain, take care of yourself." At first he paid no attention, but when the warning was repeated, inquired further of the man, and thus discovered the plot. I have had the unexpected good fortune to get hold of the ship's log book, with the nautical narrative of the affair, and have also in my possession a portion of your grandfather's private journal, commencing January 5, four days later, and containing frequent allusions to the villain. The two together enable me to present a complete history of the matter, with the feelings awakened at the very time. I begin with the entry in the ship's log.

"Thursday, 26 Jan'y. Log Book kept by John Reid, 2nd Mate. —At 8 a horrid Conspiricy was Discovered and Revealed to the Capt. by Edward Nolton, of the Mats intention, this Night, to murder the Captain and such of the Crew as would not Side with him, and take command of the Ship. This Information being confirmed by Job Farwell and Robert Bruce, the Mate then being on the forecastle, was called aft & Made a prisoner, Bound, a Centre (Sentry) Put over him. Testimony of Michael Turner, who he had made his confederat (a man who was then Separated from the Crew for having broke open & Stole Gin out of the Cargo Casks), that he meant to have killed the Captain Last Night, & stole down below at 3 o'clock this Morning with a Topmaul hid under his Jacket for that purpose, whene after putting his head into the Cabin he steped aside into his State room, where remaining a few Minutes, he hid the Maul under his bed-Clothes and came on Deck. It fortinatly happned to be Squally this Night, and the Captain, after keeping the deck until one o'clock, went down, but did not turn in. Job Caswill declared that at 8 A.M., when at the wheele, the Mate came to him, showed him an Invoice of the Cargo, and told him he Ment to kill the Captain & take the command. This man had sailed with him before, which was the reason of his trusting him with his intention. He tried to persuade him from his wicked design. He had Endeavoured to gain Several of the People to Side with him, without telling them anything more than they should fare better & be at no allowance. At 4 A.M., he disengaged himself and ran aloft, forward. Called to know if the Captain would for Give him, or he would jump overboard. To this no reply was made. At daylight Saill was Shortened, and I went up with two men to Bring him down, when he droped overboard. The small Boat was hoisted out; he soon swam towards the ship and was towed on Board. A shed was built at the Qr deck bulk-head, Under Which he was chained by both legs.

"It appeared that there was some discontent amongst the Crew from hard duty, and being at Allowance, altho the Latter was a very Large one; Besides which, one half of the Peoples chests had been ordred put below, to make room & give air in the Steerage. This they appeared to be Dissatisfied with. The Mate, therefore, calculated that the most part were ready to Undertake aney Mischeif he should sett them about. As for himself he had much neglected his duty, and Slept Allways in his watch, in which situation he was several times Caught by the Captain & several reprimands. Last Sunday the Captain found him again asleep, the weather Squally, the wind had shifted, and the ship going 8 points from her course. After putting the ship about he called the Carpenter & put him in the Mate's watch, to see that a good look out was kept. From this Moment, it is supposed, he was detarmnd in his horrid design, as he got a spare harpoon & fitted it in a short staff about four feet long, altho there was a harpoon properly fitted for use, and the one he put a handle on could be of no service for striking fish; had likewise said to several of the People that it was no Crime to Kill a person. From the whole of the information of this astonishing circumstance, it appears that this ill-guided young man supposed it would be an Easey matter to possess himself of the Ship & Cargo, in those Seas, without any Risque of being Brought to Justice. Had been Inquesative to know of me the number of Shot on board, and about three weeks ago told Job Casewell he expected to see the guns all mounted are the Passage was at an end. He now appears to be anctious to Know whether this Plot will cost him his Life, and to be very Penitent."

The captain's orders, in this critical moment, were given by him with pistols in hand, and the accomplices of the mate were so intimidated by the stern bearing of their commander that they did not venture on resistance. Of the anxieties of the next three months, the account is best given in my father's own words, and I quote from his private journal. These extracts have been considerably extended beyond my first plan. On reading the journals it has seemed to me that they not only present vivid descriptions of his sea life, but bring out, very forcibly, marked features of his character. The entries were jotted down, from day to day, for his own use, intended for no other eye, and have the life and freshness of the actual present. They are real, undisguised, expressions of his feelings, noted at the instant. No one after reading them can mistake the man. I only wish they had been all preserved. As it is there are only fragments.

"January 30, 1792.—Peace and good order appears to be well established, with a visible dread of displeasing me marked on the countenances of the men, or rather an ardent wish to please, with a fear of falling short. I am now in the situation of an absolute prince whose authority is strengthened by the discovery of a plot to overset it."

"Feb. 4th, 1792.—At day-break saw a ship which fired a gun to leeward and hoisted Portuguese colours. At 8 I spoke her, and sent the small boat aboard with a cheese as a present, and to desire the captain to receive my bad subject on board. The boat returned and brought me four bottles of port wine, but would not comply with my request. This ship is from Lisbon, bound to Brazil, equipped like a sloop of war with nearly 100 men on board."

"Feb. 5.—On an examination of water, found full 1000 gallons on board. This will enable me to proceed on to the Isle of France (Mauritius), without stopping at the Cape of Good Hope, although I wish it for the purpose of putting my bad subject out of the ship. However deserving of punishment he is, yet ironed and confined as it is requisite to keep him, I heartily wish him from the ship, and his situation enlarged."

"Feb. 8th.—Moderate and cloudy. For several days I have derived some amusement from making netting and ornamenting the ship. The mind is never in a better trim than when occupied, although trifles are the object." (As illustrative of the disposition shown by the above entry, I remark that during this period of conscious insecurity and danger, I find occasional notices of his cat, his pigeons, etc., showing how he could divert himself in the midst of his anxieties.)

Feb. 19.—Referring to means of ascertaining his position, —"Can receive no aid from lunar observations, having no assistants, and the minute hand of the watch being broken. But these things are more thought of in general than they merit, for we know that old Drake hobbled round Cape Horn, and the Portugüese doubled the Cape of Good Hope, neither of whom had better instruments than a country carpenter could make in an hour."

"Feb. 22.—A smart breeze of wind from the N.E. Everything appears to go well of late, and I feel quite easy and happy."

"March 3.—I begin to reap the advantages of discipline and good order. The crew are cheerful, obedient, and the major part with a great degree of acquired activity. The space of one minute is allotted for relieving the watch, and none permitted to lie down or sleep whilst on watch, under penalty of relieving the cook."

"March 12.—For near three weeks I have been a good deal out of trim, owing, I presume, to the deranged state of my stomach. It just now stands me in hand to attend particularly to my health; it is indeed the first time in my life that I ever felt anxious about it."

"March 13.—I was informed that there was much uneasiness in the steerage proceeding from one of the crew being determined to reveal the secrets of others who were knowing to the mate's plot, on which I wrote a billet and sent it to be nailed up in the steerage. The purport was forbidding any person from making known to me any mischief past, forgiving offenders, with severe threats against any who should conceal villainy hereafter. It hurts me to see the unhappy—and otherwise it is impolitic to have men in dread and their hands at liberty."

"March 14.—The mean result of three azimuths gave the variation 13°4′ W. Agreeably to the variation chart, this gives me fifty leagues ahead of the ship, a circumstance which I am heartily glad of. If the chart is exact this leaves me but 240 leagues from the Cape, where I have now determined to touch, if easily practicable, for the purpose of clearing the ship of her deck lumber, and lumber of another nature, which is as unpleasing as dangerous for me to retain on board. I have frequently heard several mates of vessels in the India trade, from Philadelphia, much censured for their arbitrary proceedings towards their crews, and particularly by my worthy and respectable owner. There may be some instances which merit it, but commonly 'tis the reverse. I now owe the safety of my ship and life to discipline. I feel conscious of having acquitted my duty with the utmost humanity towards my ship's company, and I presume but for one or two scabbed sheep there never would have been any uneasiness amongst them."

"March 20.—This afternoon the 2nd mate mentioned his fears lest some of the people who had been concerned or knowing to F.'s conspiracy should liberate him, as they themselves were afraid of being brought to justice, that they were at variance amongst themselves, threatening one the other's life. Indeed, never I believe was there so large a proportion of rascals on board any vessel, but if this wind continues I will rid me of two or three of the most mischievous, by either setting them on shore at the Cape, or going into the harbor and putting them on board a man-of-war. The equinox is much against this last course. At noon Cape of Good Hope, S. 80 E., distant 80 leagues."

"March 22.—Fresh breezes, with showers of rain. Saw gulls, albatrosses and whales, indications of the vicinity of land. I suspect villainy in the steerage, although I have been very particular in my orders the last 24 hours. There is some plot.

my agent informs me, amongst the three or four that are afraid of being punished, but what it is he does not know; I am well prepared."

"March 23.—Squally, with unsettled weather, in the evening—bent a cable and got all clear for going into harbor for the purpose of getting rid of my bad subject. I gave permission to the 2nd mate to speak to F., and tell him if he had anything to say in his defence, he might write me, on which he sent me a paper imploring mercy, with a full acknowledgment of his crime. I forgive him, and trust his future conduct will not abuse this lenity. I shall therefore set him on shore with a couple of his accomplices, that they may go and try their fortune elsewhere."

Extracts from the ship's log-book: "March 26.—I this day observed to the Captain that it was Probable sum attempts would Be Made to get C. F. clar by sum of the crew, which keeping him on Board was dangerous."

"March 28.—C. F. having addressed the Captain in a supplicating manner, he sent me to said F. to tell him that if there was anything to lessen the enormity of his crime he had full liberty to write. This message I Delivered, and he wrote a petition, on which the Captain sent me to tell him, his Life should be Spared."

"March 29.—Moderate and cloudy. At sunset five leagues distant from the land. At 5 o'clock hoisted out the yawl, rigged and victualled her for a fortnight, released C. F., and gave him twenty dollars, with which he put off from the ship to the shore about four leagues from us, and about six to the N. of Saldanha harbor, and twenty from Table Bay. He appeared to be exceedingly grateful for this indulgence. The reason of the boat being provisioned for so long a time was that he might avail of favorable opportunity on one of the small islands for getting to Table Bay, without stopping at Saldanha, where possibly the Dutch soldiers would stop him."

"Extract from ship's log: March 29.—At 5 Tacked Ship. C. F., chief Mate, having fully confessed his Crime and Requested the Small Boat to go on shore in, she was this Morning Given him with Sails and a fortnight's Provision, with twenty Dolars in Cash. With the which went from along side, with a Pleasant Breess from the Shore. The Land about 6 Leagues from Saldanha Harbor, E.S.E., 4 Leagues From the Land."

This was equivalent to sparing the conspirator's life, as his crime was a capital one. I cannot but notice the kind consideration shown for this bad man, and that at a time when my father was obliged to exercise the utmost vigilance against similar nefarious plots. It seems that he was sent away alone. The man made good his escape and return to America, and within my remembrance was living in comfortable circumstances in Philadelphia. My father, having thus disposed of the ringleader, gave up his intention of going into the harbor at the Cape and continued his voyage to Mauritius.

"April 14.—The steward sold the contents of the late mate's chest at the mast, in which was found the commencement of a journal beginning thus: 'Everything goes on very well. I have many strange thoughts come into my mind, the like of which I never felt before.'"

"April 19.—The steward informed me that there was some movement amongst part of the crew concerned with F., who were afraid of being brought to justice on arrival in port. Several of them had separately asked him if I was turned in, and for several preceding days had been whispering together, the second mate and carpenter being of the number. In consequence I took proper methods to prevent any villainy. My fears were chiefly for three well-affected men in the steerage, who, together with the cook and steward, are all I can depend on, but should my lads attempt anything, they'll probably catch a Tartar or take a Scotch prize."

"April 21.—My head out of trim with faint turns. The last of my poor pigeons disappeared this morning, whose loss I deplore with all the sorrow of a pet-monger."

These two extracts, from the same page, exhibit a remarkable contrast.

"April 25.—Employ is certainly a most excellent preventive against falling into mischief. I observe that the re-establishment of my health has made some demure countenances, and I'll find plenty of work to preserve them a second time from temptation."

"April 29.—Weather as yesterday, and at night much rain, with thunder and lightning. I caught 300 gallons of water, which is a seasonable supply. In consequence of this acquisition, I ordered puddings and beans to be given to the crew alternately every day, the scurvy having claimed acquaintance with several of them. It being near a month since I got anything fresh, I to-day dined sumptuously off a roasted ship-rabbit, called by the vulgar ashore, rat. The flesh of this animal is exceedingly delicate, and I am astonished that epicureans have not tolerated them at table."

"May 2.—This makes five months since my leaving port,

debarred from society, and shut up with a gang of wretches the major part of whom are deterred from villainy by dread."

Two notes in the Journal for May 3 are very interesting, the first as an allusion, almost solitary, to the feelings of his early naval life,—the second as a revelation of the tenderness of heart and warmth of affection hidden under an outwardly stern deportment. "In the morning a large ship to the southward, edging towards us with *English colors*. Ten years" (I think this is a mistake for nine,) "and some days are now past since that under thee my young blood glowed for conquest and honest fame, when at the side of my early friend I felt all that martial ardor could inspire; but, alas! with him are buried every dear idea of falling on the deck of fame."

"I set about arranging my papers with reluctance, but in this examination, which I would willingly have avoided, what an unlooked-for, happy surprise!—a lock of my dear worthy patron's hair, inclosed in papers which he delivered to me for my perusal. How little did I then suppose they contained this invaluable mark of his affection! Every nobler feeling of my soul is in motion."

The person mentioned with such strong feeling must, I think, have been his brother Thomas. Who the early friend could have been I have no means of discovering. The ship proved to be an East Indiaman. "Two of the officers came on board, and in the course of conversation, enquired after Messrs. Russell & Brick, on behalf of a Mrs. Sheppard, passenger on board their vessel. I remembered having a letter to the address of this lady, which I delivered. This rencounter might be considered an extraordinary event on a small scale. It encouraged me to ask after my cousin, Lt. J. Goldsworthy, at Madras, but without equal fortune."

"May 6.—I this night kept the deck, during which one of the good seamen had an opportunity to tell me that he had overheard some talk amongst the mutineers, expressing their fears of being brought to punishment,—that the second mate, etc., were present, and at best expected to be turned ashore. He further gave me to understand that some time back they had investigated the cargo, and concluded there was a large sum of money on board, in addition, to purchase cargo, and that this had been no small inducement for them to conclude to give me the coup de grace."

"May 7.—Squally, unsettled weather. Got all clear for immediate anchoring in case of danger in the night. At meridian an ill-natured cloud stepped betwixt me and the sun, which leaves me to guess at the latitude. Last evening, at six o'clock, went below for the purpose of refreshing myself, being extremely fatigued, intending to rise at eight and keep the deck until morning, as I had the night before. I waked at hearing the watch called, and going on deck found to my great astonishment, it was four in the morning. This is the longest nap I ever remember taking, and at a moment when, for more causes than one, I ought not to have closed my eyes. All's well that ends well."

"May 9.—At sunset saw three small islands, situated off the N. W. end of the Isle of France, which I passed betwixt at midnight, the moon shining bright, and by ten was within a league of my port, when the wind took me ahead. It is now favorable, and I trust will enable me safely to harbor this night."

This arrival terminated more than three months of imminent, hourly peril from his treacherous crew. The next entry in the

Journal is dated the day of his leaving the Isle de France, July 7, 1792. During his stay in port, he shipped new officers and crew, and made preparation for a sealing voyage, his destination being Cape Horn. He remarks that the masters of the American vessels were on board at his departure. "My acquaintance took leave with three cheers, and I stood out to sea, to commence a circumnavigating voyage which promises a duration of two years. Attend, my good genius. I will either succeed or bid farewell to cares."

"July 8.—Variable winds and weather. I now made a general muster and found 36 on board, including myself, composed of ¼ English, ½ French, and ¼ Spaniards,—a motley crew, but appearing good, with good officers. The 1st mate, English, the 2nd French, 3rd English, and two French midshipmen. I discharged and turned ashore, at the Isle de France, six of my bad subjects. The remainder, whom I brought out, continue in the vessel. I have now a numerous but not expensive crew. Staten Land will, in three months, probably furnish 'em with employ in procuring seal-skins and oil. The destruction of my brother amphibious animals will create many painful sensations. Man, what escapes thy avarice?"

"July 9.—Saw the volcano on the Island of Bourbon, bearing S.W., about 20 leagues distant."

The ship ran down the Mozambique channel, between the African coast and Madagascar. For insubordination, two of the crew were put in irons. The Journal for July 28, notes: "The men in confinement being ironed on the after part of the quarter-deck appeared so pensive, void of malice, and pinched with cold from the chilliness of the wind that pity induced me to order their release, and the ship's company to be called to the quarter-deck. I then addressed a few words to them, pointing out the ill consequences of neglect of duty and disrespect to their officers; that I forgave the late prisoners, and in future if any man had cause of complaint to apply to me, and he should be redressed, but hereafter insubordination would be punished with severity.

"At sunset I had a good view of the land, and by the chart found myself abreast of Muscle Bay, Cape Delgado, bearing N.W., 10 leagues. It is but 48 hours since I was opposite the first point of Natal, which lies 100 leagues to the N.E., and by log have not made above 35° S., so that the current in that time has set me 160 miles. If I was to speak of this extraordinary circumstance I should be supposed to take the privilege of a traveller."

"Aug. 21.—I this morning set the carpenter at work cutting out ports for the waist guns. I purpose piercing her for sixteen, although I have but half that number on board. What signifies it? Nine-tenths of mankind are but half what they appear to be, and on the voyage on which I am bound it may be of consequence to appear formidable."

"Aug. 25.—The ship's company having last Sunday been deficient in clean shirts and shaving, they were in consequence told they would lose their wine for the week in future when dirty. I to-day had the satisfaction of seeing a clean, healthy-looking set of fellows."

"Aug. 27.—Fresh breezes, with squalls at intervals. I flatter myself that in this latitude (2[illegible]° S.) I shall have the heavy trade. I am the first ship that ever doubled the Cape of Good

Hope to go round Cape Horn. I feel confident that by this northern track I shall arrive at Staten Land earlier than if I had taken the bull by the horns, gone into high latitudes, wrecked my ship and debilitated the crew with the scurvy."

"Aug. 28.—In the morning my lad G. came to acquaint me that Cornwall, a favorite of mine, had been wrangling with one of the French sailors, for which Mr. Le Fort had beat him, and was going to put him in irons. I went on deck, and on enquiry it appeared that the Frenchman was in the wrong. The officer said that Cornwall had been insolent to him. As I suspected some malice, I only reprimanded the man and sent him away. This so exasperated Mr. Le Fort that he went to his cabin, though he resumed his duty on the next watch. He is a good officer, but a fiery, tyrannical man, on whom I must keep a check. As I enforce respect and obedience from men to officers, so I will as absolutely exact humanity to inferiors as deference to superiors."

"Aug. 29.—A light trade wind at E. This morning, Louise, wife of Malbrook, was delivered of six lovely puppies, to the no small joy of that illustrious and amiable couple."

"Aug. 30.—In the evening an American sailor came to make a complaint against some French, and in the morning French against American. I had strictly forbid all national reflections, from which these disputes arise, and in consequence wrote the following memorandum and caused it to be fixed against the bulk-head, in French and English."

"1. As frequent complaints have been made of wrangling amongst the crew, by each other, they are herewith forbid, under penalty of being put in irons, in future to use any aggravating language or gestures, or to cast any national reflections.

"2. All who are not satisfied on board may leave the ship at the Brazils, and those who behave ill shall absolutely be turned ashore.

"3. If there are any two men inveterate against each other and wishing to fight, they shall have permission so to do, on condition of fighting for the space of half an hour; and if either gives out sooner, he shall be brought to the shrouds and receive one dozen lashes from the other."

This somewhat original peace edict seems to have proved effectual.

"Sept. 17.—I now devote part of my attention to teaching my lad George the mathematics. His dutiful behaviour during my last passage, when every species of villainy was exerted to corrupt him, merits my affection and services."

"Sept. 18.—Fresh meat once a week to the crew. They continue in good health, for although thirty-five on board, and upwards of seventy days at sea, there is not one incapable of doing duty. Their national animosities have subsided since they had my conditional permission to fight, and there now appears to be a general tranquillity on board. Tremendous thunder and lightning at midnight. A clap so near as to terrify the watch, who supposed the ship struck. The lightning conductor was at the mast-head, but as the people were momentarily blinded by the flash, they could not see whether it descended by it or no."

By October the latitude of 40° S. had been reached, and the crew began to suffer from cold. The kindliness of the commander appears in the journal for Oct. 2.

"Being informed this morning that several of the sailors were without bedding I ordered my cabin-locker cushions to be served out for beds, and had canvass cover-lids made, there being no woollen for that purpose. It is ten months since I left Boston during which I have been eight months at sea. No one can accuse me with justice of letting my ship catch the scurvy for want of exercise."

"Oct. 6.—Horrid cold pinching weather with hail and heavy squalls which after 4 P.M. obliged me to lay to under a mizzen stay sail and to haul down that at intervals."

"Oct. 13.—Saw a number of seals, penguins etc. Appointed the whale-boats their crews and set them to fitting out their gear, as I probably may soon have occasion for them. Indeed to-day had they been ready I should have made a whaling commencement for the purpose of dissipating my present inactive time, as well as in consideration of profit."

"Oct. 15.—I now feel impatient to get on the other side, (of Cape Horn). It is now 100 days since I left the Isle de France, 269 of my being at sea, and making but one harbor. In clearing out was found a couple of shot slung by a short piece of ratling each, said to be done by the French sailors to effect the destruction of their English shipmates about six weeks ago when quarrels prevailed. I was likewise acquainted with other villainous intentions tending to the same purpose which had I known at the time would have led me to punish with severity, but as it is shall pass it in silence."

"Oct. 16.—W. of Falkland Islands. Towards midnight blowing a fresh gale brought me under close-reefed topsails. At 3 it hove up black to the westward,—in a few minutes blew with great violence. Fortunately I had hauled up the mainsail and got in the mizzen topsail, as it was near twenty minutes before the watch below came on deck, their clothes wet and weather extremely cold. Took in all sail but the foresail and wore ship. She to my great comfort lying off shore. At 6 the gale had moderated."

"Oct. 17.—Stood on a wind to the S.W., until 5 P.M., when having passed the islands and flattering myself with a good night's run towards Staten Land, breakers and a low sandy island were seen a head, on which I hauled and stood to the N. Soon after 8 it came on to blow and by midnight brought me under my foresail, which it was necessary to hand soon after for its security. As the wind was to the W. and the ship off shore I had nothing to apprehend but from its shifting."

I copy a little more from the log book to show the anxiety and discomfort of navigating those stormy seas with the imperfect equipments and charts of the last century.

"Moderated sufficiently to set close reefed topsails. Stood for Port Egmont with an intention to make a harbor for supplies and to remain until the wind shifted. At meridian squally, saw the land, having been curranted near twenty miles to the E. since the evening."

"Oct. 18.—Fresh gales and squally. At 2 was within four or five miles of the land, but having no exact description of it, and an imperfect manuscript chart, could not ascertain it. As it blew too fresh to work the ship, or send a boat to examine did not think it prudent to run in, the land within being a long low yellow island. Came to a determination to bear away and pass to the E. of the Falkland Islands. At 6 was abreast of what I judged to be Cape Tamar, and continued on my course for Cape Dolphin. The mates were of opinion that the land was the eastermost of the Falkland Islands and the opening within was not Byron's Sound, but then we must have been amazingly curranted. I continued to stand for Cape Dolphin which is said to be but eight leagues from the last mentioned cape, and ran half that distance without seeing it or the Eddystone rock, and now began to relax in my opinion and was persuaded to haul to the S. At 8 I brought to, not thinking it prudent to run and likewise purposing to look into Barclay Sound to procure some supplies from the Spaniards. Lay off and on during the night and in the morning bore away in quest of the land. Soon after a large rock was seen bearing N.E. and directly after Cape Dolphin made its appearance. I now repented of my want of firmness having lost a night's run, there being yet twenty leagues to make to arrive at the place where I supposed myself."

There is now a gap in the journal until February, 1793, and then only a single page. The interval of four months must have been chiefly spent at Staten Land or vicinity in whaling and sealing. The journal resumes:

"Unsettled weather with showers of rain and winds from W. to S.W. At 8 A.M. the wind drawing out the mouth of the harbor I began to unmoor, at half past came to sail and in ten minutes was clear of this dangerous harbor, though not without considerable risk. Directly after it came on to blow. Clewed down and sent away a boat to bring on board another which had got adrift at the entrance. Hove up the anchor which yet remained towing with fifteen feet of cable. By meridian stowed the anchors, hoisted in the boats and bore away to the E."

"Variable winds. At 2 P.M. brought to off Squally Cove, and sent in the English boat for the clothes of two seamen who had exchanged berths with two of my people, who were yet desirous to try their fortunes in this inhospitable country. Three vessels belonging to New York soon after came out bound home, one of which I soon after spoke, and all of which I had written by. At 4 the boat returned, discharged her with some few presents, and sent on shore my Indian man Friday to reside at the Factory until opportunity presented itself for returning him to his native woods. The wind became light with rain and having the flood against me I remained between Cook's island and the Main until 9 o'clock, when the ebb tide swept me away to the E. At 5 A.M. a smart gale came butt end from the S.W. Bore away and at sunrise Staten Land bore S.W. by S. 15 leagues. Adieu inhospitable country. May snow, rocks and marine animals be in future thy only companions. Unbent and stowed away cables. My ship sails well and is exceeding stiff."

This is the close of the captain's private log. It would have been interesting to be able to trace this eventful voyage to a happy conclusion. It would appear that the original plan was to proceed to the N.W. coast of America and to return home by the East Indies, making it, as called in the journal on leaving Isle de France, a circumnavigation of the globe, a rare achievement in those days. One of the last entries before reaching the harbor at Staten Land is: "Indeed if I can easily procure a cargo of oil and about 15 or 20000 seal skins then I shall abandon the N.W. project." As the project was abandoned I presume the ship was successfully laden at Staten Land, and from thence returned directly to her port in the U. S., either Boston or New York.

There is another fragment of a journal, kept on a voyage from New York to China, from Jan'y 21, 1796, to May 20th. This was his final voyage, with the exception of the trip to France after his marriage. His growing dislike of a sea-faring life is repeatedly expressed in the previous voyage, viz.:

"March 19, 1792.—I have been out of trim for this fortnight past and followed a course of bark and now feel much better. Indeed I never had more occasion for robust health, which for these last eighteen months has not been altogether as it formerly was. I am sensible to fatigue—the sea less agreeable. Fame and money are the common objects of pursuit on it, neither of which can procure me the shadow of that happiness which would result from the possession of my little girl, books and solitude. Return thou wanderer. Already hast thou partaken of a large proportion of fortune's acid and known enough of the world."

"Aug. 10, 1792.—Wind N. with great humidity in the air, to which I have become very sensible, rheumatic pains on the least variation in the weather. It is certain that I have seen my best sea days and that I ought to retire, which I trust the present voyage will enable me to do."

His purpose to retire was overcome, and on the 21st January, 1796, he again set sail. He finds on this voyage much to complain of in his crew and still more in his officers. He issued to the first Mate written rules of conduct of a very decided character, in which he says, "The ship's duty must be carried on with spirit. Where exertion is required an officer's hand must be foremost. The sailors are to be treated with humanity but never spoken to unless on duty. The deck must be relieved in five minutes after the watch is called, and in uncertain weather no person is to undress when below. 'Tis a sensible gratification to me to see others happy which I shall endeavour to promote as far as consistent with the duty I owe my employers, but an officer materially deviating from the regulations herewith specified can't but be miserable." He had soon occasion to display his usual firmness.

"Feb. 7.—The sailors much addicted to sleeping on their watch, and the Mate informs me that several have lately been intoxicated, in consequence of which I sent the steward with orders to them to deliver the rum up to him. The steward reported that the men had not given him any liquor. He was sent again, when some of them bluntly refused to deliver it up and were determined to keep it at all events. Rum is a cursed thing at sea, especially in a ship bound on a long voyage where sailors too frequently consider themselves at liberty to give the law. Desirous to avoid anything serious, but determined to carry my point, I postponed coercive measures till 4 o'clock to give time for reflection, and the steward, who is a very prudent young man, was directed to use persuasion with them as coming from himself. They were resolved to keep it. At 4 I ordered the Mate to send all hands on the quarter deck, where, after preparing two cases of pistols which I left below, I went myself, pointed out to them the impropriety of their conduct which further disobedience would compel me to punish with the utmost severity, peremptorily ordered them to lay their keys on the binnacle, which was submissively complied with. The Mate and carpenter were sent into the forecastle to examine their chests, from which they took about ten gallons. The crew were then dismissed with wholesome advice, seasoned with a few threats. One of them I understood hove his liquor overboard to prevent losing possession of it."

"Feb. 14.—In the morning found the sails much colored with a reddish dust that gave them the appearance of being tinged with bark. The same thing happened to me last voyage when near the Equator, and even fowls, killed the night before and exposed to the weather, had the appearance, when brought to the table, of having been saltpetred. This heavy penetrating oppressive air sets me out of trim and my old rheumatic complaints cry out. Poor unfortunate that I am to be again enticed to expose myself to vicissitudes of climate and to being eaten by sharks, when I had sufficient to subsist comfortably on in a cottage. Man with all his boasted reason is the most senseless and inconsistent of the animal creation."

"Feb. 17.—To-day I cut out an awning for the quarter-deck to guarantee the ship's company as much as possible against the ardor of the sun, whose influence I expect shortly to feel very sensibly under the Equator. I have lately approached it with rapidity, making a run of 712 miles in four days, although on a wind. The crossing trade winds is probably the most pleasing navigation on the seas. Neither tack nor sheet has been started during the last three days although the ship has been under a cloud of sail."

"March 1.—A complaint was made by the cook that one of the sailors had used him in a shameful manner. The offender was of that description of lawless men who delight in mischief and who had been reprimanded by me some time ago for bad behaviour. I have ever found that where good advice and lenient measures fail coercive ones are salutary. 'Tis an ungrateful task to punish but a man must do his duty, and whoever neglects it becomes a partaker in the offence or crime. I would have ordered the fellow in irons for a spell of reflection, but his labour was wanted. I therefore sent for him on the quarter deck and with a smart hickory stick bountifully bestowed all the strength of my arm on his bones. Should his memory otherwise be weak I think this will recall the affair to his mind for at least a month to come. When a man has an unpleasing business of this nature that he can't possibly let pass he ought to do it so effectually as to impress a dread on his ship's company."

"March 2.—At midnight observed the Great Bear, or pointers to the North Star, to be considerably above the horizon and in the Southern hemisphere two spots commonly called the Magellan clouds, but as they are of a fixed consistency in the heavens 'tis obvious they are of a very different matter. There are three, one white and two black. One of the latter is not yet perceptible."

(These remarkable nebulæ are now engaging the intense study of astronomers, as among the most interesting of celestial bodies.)*

* "It appears a noteworthy circumstance that near the centre of the great Southern rich region are found those two wonderful objects called the Magellanic clouds, vast globe-shaped conglomerations, in which are contained not only myriads of stars of all orders of magnitude after the seventh, but also every kind of star cloudlet."—*Proctor, the Expanse of Heaven, page 268.*

"Successful in sail making, but this morning cutting out a jib with the last cloth I perceived that I was wrong with the foot-gore. The discovery was fortunately made in time and I remedied the fault privately in my cabin. If it had not fixed on me a degree of ridicule by the sailors, 'twould at least have lessened their opinion of my abilities. Any man in the station of an officer must be exceeding circumspect before his inferiors to show himself equal to what he undertakes. A superiority in all marine affairs never fails to inspire respect, or inability derision, and forecastle wit is sometimes severe."

"March 9.—Ship in good order, crew tolerably well disciplined, alert and passively obedient, everybody in good health and the wind uncommonly favorable considering the ship is but just on the Tropic. And yet I am not happy. 'Tis a line of life I am weary of and anxiously anticipate its termination. Am tired of being a despot and finding fault. How strange is that passion for power that betrays men to the perpetration of the most unnatural actions! In my early days a large proportion of ambition fell to my share, but now no more remains than what is requisite to stimulate me to my duty, which duty, I trust, after the voyage I am now on will consist in a due observance of tenderness for my little girl, affection for my friends and an independent but moderate patriotism for the country of which I am a citizen. I flatter myself with retiring from busy life and in a solitude not over austere passing the remainder of a life, that hitherto has been a succession of enterprise, fatigue and chagrin."

"March 13.—Yesterday reading a book containing a catalogue of memorable events with the dates, &c., the following inconsistency attracted my attention:—

'1451 years, A.C.—The Jews settled themselves in the conquered country of Canaan, and began to observe the Sabbatical year.

'1406 A.C.—Iron was discovered from the accidental burning of the woods of Mt. Ida in Crete.'

Pray Mr. Historian, condescend to inform me with what kind of weapons did the Jews subdue their enemies. The Bible tells us that they smote them with the edge of the sword."

"March 22.—Fresh gales with considerable of a sea. Had the misfortune to lose my horse-radish garden over the stern—spoiled by the ship's scudding aft and dipping it in salt water. This evil is a very partial one as I have plenty of that article on board. Besides, altho' two months at sea, I have onions, potatoes and garlic in abundance. Had former navigators paid attention to these things how many lives would they have saved by stopping the ravages of scurvy among their ship's companies. Anson tells us that he lost one-half of his crew in doubling Cape Horn. I think he would have been rightly served to have the Cape doubled on him for his neglect or want of thought in not providing such anti-scorbutics as would have effectually guaranteed 'em against the horrors of that disorder, and which would have been attended with but very trifling expense."

"March 23.—At midnight the Mate waked me with the information that one of the watches, or half the ship's company, had got into a drunken frolic and had possession of the forecastle, threatening destruction to any that would attempt to come forward. I instantly rose and re-primed my pistols, by which time I was told that they were all hands fighting among themselves. I therefore concluded it prudent as it was night, the weather dirty and fellows crazy, to let them punish each other, ordering all the sober ones on the quarter-deck and vowing a severe flogging to the rioters when the morning should have restored 'em to their senses. At breakfast I ordered them to be sent aft. The poor obedient wretches appeared like thieves before justice. Their faces horribly bruised and their air of penitence softened the resentment I felt against them as disturbers of order and good discipline, and instead of the cat and nine tails prepared I ordered vinegar to wash their faces, and dismissed 'em without a reprimand. The means of their being thus intoxicated proceeded from liquor that had been taken from them six weeks ago, part of which I had lately ordered to be restored." (This was done as an intended kindness on account of the change from equatorial heat to chilling winds as they ran into high latitudes.) "In consequence of this abuse of confidence directions were issued to take from them what remained, which together with the part in my possession was thrown overboard. I believe the lads thought themselves well acquit in not suffering otherwise than in their dear grog."

"March 26.—I begin to have serious thoughts of going into the Cape of Good Hope, being apprehensive that if I proceed to the Isle of France, I shall either find it in a state of blockade or my detention there will bring me too late in the China sea."

"April 2.—At 5 had a most severe thunder gust. Fortunately all the light sails were handed and heavy ones clewed down. It blew with great violence but the ship flying before it lessened considerably its force. A vein of wind passed at about two cables' length on the ship's starboard of whose force it is difficult to judge, but the white foam it made induces me to suppose it

French privateer. This gentleman was overjoyed to see me and recounted to a person present the circumstance I have mentioned. He then informed me that his brother had touched in there about two months ago on his way to New York, having relinquished his employ as chief of the Dutch Presidency at China, and that he was going to reside in America—that since my seeing him he had been ambassador from the States of Holland to Pekin and had now retired with a very ample fortune. I felt great satisfaction at this intelligence as he is a very worthy man, and probably that pleasure was somewhat increased with the expectation of recovering two thousand dollars for extra services undertaken for the recovery of his property, due Mr. Jones and me. As this is a debt of honor or rather gratitude a man of property would be supposed to discharge it more cheerfully than one in mediocre circumstances. The Baron then, (we being alone) gave me a long detail of public matters, censured the pusillanimity of his fellow-citizens and concluded by regretting the loss of his place, being one of the government.

In the morning I went to see Commodore Blanket. The old man in his manners represented my worthy old commander, is about sixty-five and much weather-beaten. He condescended to ask me to take a seat on his sofa, altho' a Lieutenant stood at a respectful distance, cap in hand, without daring to meet the old Tar's eyes when addressed by him. The old gentleman as well as the General was very particular in his enquiries about America and *Mr.* Washington. He asked me for newspapers and I promised to send him a packet. Now one of my principal objects for seeing the old man was to get his permission to embark some Swedish sailors, of whom 150 were here, their ship having been cast away in Table Bay. I had been formerly acquainted with the unfortunate Captain and he readily assented to my taking them. The Commodore had made application to him for some of them which was refused, and in consequence would not let them enter on board any other vessel. Thinking that the old veteran in his good humor, w^d not refuse me, I respectfully made my solicitation but was deceived." (This "ancient mariner" was "full of strange oaths" which I take the liberty of omitting.)—"His reply was, 'Oh, sir, I smoke you, you are I find put in here to get men are you? No, sir, not a man, and if you take any, your bondsman that you'll have to get before your departure will have to pay 500 dollars for each.' I quickly mollified the old boy, by assuring him that I possessed too much respect for his orders, as well as veneration for his person, to disobey the former, that I had conceived those foreigners beneath his notice. 'However,' said he, 'there is an Italian lying where your ship is, bound, I understand, to the Isle de France. If you can get his men you may and welcome.' This singular indulgence I thanked him for, and the old gentleman without doubt supposed he had conferred a favor on me by giving me leave to distress another which he had no business with. I withdrew leaving him in a good temper and doing me the unexpected honor of rising and accompaning me to the door.

Finding nothing was to be done here I went to the Baron's and passed the evening and set off at daybreak for my ship, with a miserable horse, about the size of an ass, which fell with me three times on the road. Found that an English sixty-four, and six Dutch prizes, had come round from Table Bay, one of which having struck on a rock was run aground in the cove, where she filled with water having on b^{d} a cargo of pepper, &c., valued at £60,000 sterling. The accident I presume was no unpleasant sight for the Dutchmen.

P.M. The ship's water being completed I got on board a dozen sheep and sundry other stock. At sunset an American ship arrived, which I learnt was the Eliza of Boston from China bound home, by whom I was informed that the Malays were extremely troublesome & dangerous. Out of this ship I got a pair of four pounders, 1 cwt of powder and four black men. In the morning went on board the Ruby, (64) Capt'n Spanger. He appeared to be a polite, well behaved man, and desired me to tell the Captain of the Eliza that he wanted to see his papers. I accordingly went in search of him but found he was gone for Cape Town. I concluded it necessary to go again on b^{d} the Ruby to apologize for his neglect, when I found that Capt. Spanger was already acquainted with it and appeared to be much enraged at what he considered an insult, or at least disrespect. I said what I thought would have a tendency to soften him, but to no purpose. He instantly ordered an officer with a file of Marines to go and take possession of the ship, and not to suffer any communication with the shore or any body to go out of her. At that time my powder, guns and men were yet on board her. On my representing the circumstance he ordered my boat to be admitted. There might appear some degree of severity in Capt'n S's conduct towards the Eliza, but I had every reason to be pleased with him. He was much in want of men and might undoubtedly have much distressed me as near half my crew were English, but he contented himself with asking the number I had on board which he said were too few. He asked me if I did not mean to touch at any place on my way to China. I replied Yes, at Bencoolen. Looking me steady in the face he twice said, And no place else? I knew that he referred to the Isle de France, where two of my bad subjects, the young quack" (the surgeon previously referred to) "and 2nd Mate had given out on shore I was bound. These animals had already much to my satisfaction gone on shore, the former having robbed the medicine chest of one half its contents, every thing that was valuable and profitable. On the whole 'twas a good riddance.

Returning on board in the evening I found four marines in the ship to my great surprise. Demanding of the Corporal what they did there he told me his orders were to let nothing go out of the ship & that he came from the Ruby. I felt sensibly hurt at this conduct & was going on board to remonstrate with Capt Spanger when I learnt that he had gone to Cape Town. Concluding therefore that 'twas the puppy of a Lieutenant who had sent them on bd I determined to resent it by anchoring without the harbour in the morning if the wind should be ahead. But it coming fair at 5 A.M. I sent to request that the Marines might be withdrawn which was complied with, and at sunrise I got under way and stood out for sea.

I understood, while on shore, that the place might have been defended and the invaders easily repulsed, but that party spirit and cowardice together had made this valuable place an easy acquisition to the English. I asked the man with whom I kept how it was the people of the place made such a neat appearance. He replied, Provisions here cost nothing. I observed that they sold them dear to strangers. He answered, 'To be sure.'"

"May 5.—Fresh breezes and cloudy. Wind at N.E. with a prodigious humidity of the atmosphere. Rainy, disagreeable weather. My late ill-luck with winds has almost exhausted my patience having had it near ten days contrary in a place where I had the least right to expect it. Otherwise these voyages are sufficiently tedious with fair winds, but a man whose good or ill fortune depends on a blast of that variable element ought to become early a philosopher. I wish a few months back I had become sufficiently so to have quitted this vagabond profession with a moderate competency."

"May 7.—At 4 A.M. wind chopped round in a heavy squall to the S^d and promised some intermission to mind. At Merd'n got up top gallant mast and yards to improve the present favorable opportunity and get the ship into the trade winds with all possible expedition."

"May 11.—Light airs from the W^d & ship short of her log as before. This uncommon ill-luck in winds is a charge on the patience especially in a place where a heavy S.E. trade wind commonly blows. It is not only the disagremet of unprofitably doing nothing at sea, but I begin to have my fears of not getting in good season to China, in default of which I shall be exposed to all the bad weather that prevails in that sea with the shifting of the periodical trade winds."

"May 13.—Wind, weather, patience, &c., &c., as before. While scraping off the clams and grass from the ship's sides the carpenter discovered two spike holes open in the middle bend. Fortunately these were just above water and made none except in bad weather when the ship lay under, but had she been loaded a foot deeper they would have furnished very ample amusement to all hands the whole of the passage. 'Tis astonishing that carpenters or builders should be so careless when the lives of so many depend upon their attention. I remember on heaving out 'The Fair American' that five spike holes were found in the bottom, and the caulkers at Falmouth found four in 'The Patriot's' bends. The former were partially stopped with stuff sucking into them as she lay at the dock and the latter were paid over with pitch. Both of these obstructions luckily proved sufficient that one pump was a match for the water admitted, but had they (the holes) cleared themselves I presume they must have been fatal. I think if I ever go to sea again in a new ship I'll confide in no man's eyes but my own."

This Journal closes with arrival at the Isle de France, May 20, 1796. This voyage I believe was on the whole quite successful, but further records are wanting. It closed your grandfather's professional sea life. That he had become weary of the ocean—and especially of the heavy responsibilities imposed upon the commander of a vessel, is made very evident by the quotations above made from his Journal. I suppose he arrived in New York on his return voyage from China in the Spring of 1797, and then carried out his long cherished purpose of retiring from the sea, and exchanging the hardships and perils of the deep for the tranquil enjoyments of domestic life.

He was not over thirty-two years old when he made this change. In the prime of life, with his ability, experience and high reputation, there were great inducements to continue a few years longer in this calling, and every prospect of soon accumulating a large fortune. But his growing dislike of the sea is strongly expressed, the declared intentions of his brother Thomas gave reasonable assurance of future affluence, and he was now anticipating that union with your grandmother which conduced so much to the happiness of his subsequent life. His attachment to Elizabeth Leighton, "the little girl" of whom he writes so fondly in his journal of 1792, had been cherished for a number of years. He had known her from childhood. When she was only *a little girl*, as a conversation was going on in her mother's house respecting friendship, she exclaimed, "I know who is my friend, Captain Lee is my friend." There was a difference of twelve years in their ages so that she naturally looked up to the Captain with deference as well as affection. As the little girl developed into a young lady of uncommon loveliness she won the Captain's heart, and he became her nearest and dearest friend. She was remarkably suited to her husband, cheered and sustained him under the trials which he encountered, and possessed his fullest confidence. Your grandmother was distinguished for the charms of her personal appearance, as well as for mental energy and sprightliness. The marriage was solemnized in the city of Boston, by the Rev. Dr. Belknap, May 27, 1797.

Elizabeth Leighton was the daughter of John and Elizabeth Leighton of Boston. When the city was occupied by the British troops at the breaking out of the Revolutionary war, many of the inhabitants left their homes and removed for safety to the country. Among them was Mrs. John Leighton. Her place of retreat was Lunenburg, Massachusetts, a village about thirty miles distant from Boston, and there your grandmother was born September 22, 1776. This event occurred about three months after the battle of Bunker Hill, and not so long after the declaration of Independence. At a family gathering on her ninetieth birth day, the hands of her loving grandchildren decorated her arm chair with the star spangled banner, as an appropriate ornament for one whose life was coæval with that of the nation.

Her father, John Leighton, was captain of a merchant vessel, and was accidentally killed at Cape Haitien, Island of Haiti, April 16, 1784, by the fall of a piece of timber from the mast of his vessel. Her mother, Elizabeth Gorham, was related to several of the old families of Massachusetts, the Gorhams, Codmans, Phillipses and Coffins. She died in the City of Boston March 16, 1822, aged I think about seventy-five years. I have an indistinct recollection of her, appearing to me an exceedingly old person, and telling us children stories about the Indians and of things that occurred in the early history of the State.

The children of John & Elizabeth Leighton besides Elizabeth were John, born May 11, 1778, died in infancy—John, a second son, born Oct. 4, 1779, also died in infancy—Nathaniel Gorham, born February 1, 1774, who died in Calcutta, about the year 1825 or 1830. He served in the American Navy during the war of 1812, and was captured by the British and confined in the famous Dartmoor prison. After the war he went to the East Indies and married a lady in Calcutta. He served in the English Army in the Burmese war. He left one son with whom your grandmother kept up a correspondence, and who had the intention of entering the Church Ministry. Whether this was accomplished I am unable to say. As nothing has been heard from him for the last thirty years I presume he is no longer living.

Soon after his marriage Benjamin Lee purchased a fine farm in Lancaster, Massachusetts, distant about thirty miles from

Boston, and there applied himself to the cultivation of the soil with characteristic energy. He was indeed an enthusiastic farmer, entering into the work with his whole heart, and giving much time and study to agricultural improvements. At a later period he owned a large flock of fine Spanish Merino sheep. At that time what was called the Merino fever raged extensively, much to the detriment of many eager and unfortunate speculators. His venture in this line was I believe not unsuccessful—the clip of wool being very heavy, and the lambs bringing prices that would now seem fabulous. The raising of sheep naturally led to his taking an interest in woolen manufactures, and the cloth produced from his flock was of remarkably good quality. He prided himself in wearing no other and clothed his family in the same. When, during the Embargo preceding the war with Great Britain, Congress patriotically resolved to wear only cloth of home manufacture, Vice-President Gerry appeared at the Capitol in a suit made of cloth presented to him by my father, and had some difficulty in making his friends believe that his dress was not of imported fabric. However gratifying in one respect the attempt to introduce the manufacture of cloth in this country, it was by no means a pecuniary success, and if the woven fleeces of his merinos adorned your grandfather's person and his friends, they had no tendency to fill his pockets.

After entering upon domestic life your grandfather abandoned the sea, except that he made one voyage to France upon business. He was so dissatisfied with the careless management of the vessel in which he made the passage out, that he was unwilling to return as a passenger, and bought a ship to come home in.

A strong inducement was offered to him to return to a nautical life by President Adams, at the organization of the American Navy.

When the celebrated frigate Constitution was fitted out he was tendered a commission as her first Lieutenant. This would have given him a high position among our old naval Commanders. One of his reasons for declining this appointment was that, although a naturalized American Citizen, he was unwilling to be placed in a situation which might require him to fight against old England.

The death of Mrs. Jane Lee, his brother's widow, and the Cambridge property coming into his hands, led to his removal from Lancaster to Cambridge, where he resided from 1805 to 1819. With this my native place and home of my childhood are connected many dear and pleasant associations. My father was fond of the society of his friends, and visitors including many of the first men of Boston were numerous. It was a period of vehement political agitation, the struggle between the Federal and Democratic parties being at its height. My father was a strong Federalist and utterly opposed to the principles of Jefferson. I can remember the animated even angry discussions that took place. But although my father was not very measured in the expression of his political sentiments, and some of his neighbours were very conspicuous and earnest Democrats, political differences were not allowed to produce alienation. Elbridge Gerry continued always one of his intimate friends, and sometimes consulted with him on public measures. European affairs at that period were engrossing, as well as our own. Napoleon I. was Emperor, and my father was wont to speak of him as might be expected of an Englishman and a relative of William Pitt. I well remember his commenting upon the tidings of the battle of Waterloo, as he paced the room in no little excitement.

The occasion of our change of residence from Cambridge to Norwich was the unjust and oppressive conduct of the select-men of the town (as they were called) in the assessment of taxes. My father's taxes were suddenly raised about threefold, and when he objected to payment the select-men carried matters with a high hand and levied on his horses. I remember seeing him excited by this injustice in an unusual degree. That the proceedings of the select-men were unwarrantable was afterwards judicially decided, my father gaining a suit which he brought against them. But the effect upon his mind was such that he determined no longer to reside in the place. In one of his journeys passing through Norwich, Connecticut, he had been much struck with the beauty of a place which he understood was for sale. The house had been built by Mr. Vernet, a French gentleman from the West Indies. In the beginning of this century there was a good deal of commerce between Norwich and those Islands. Mr. Vernet becoming embarrassed returned to the West Indies, and was anxious to dispose of the property in Norwich. The purchase was made by my father in 1812, and my impression is that one object in his mind was to have a retreat for his family in case of the British, in the war just commenced, getting possession of Boston. The difficulty with the town officers of Cambridge arose afterwards. Then, for several successive years, the family left Cambridge in the Spring and did not return until Autumn, so that at the date of assessment he was resident and taxable in Norwich. This arrangement continued I think from

1816 to 1819 inclusive. In the mean time my father had negotiated with his next neighbour, Andrew Craigie, for the purchase of a large tract of land in Genessee County, New York, in part payment for which the Cambridge estate was given. These lands, containing about 15,000 acres, were part of a larger parcel known as "The Craigie Tract." The lots had been already sold to actual settlers, but only paid for in part. Thus my father's connection with Cambridge came to an end and I do not think he ever saw it afterwards. He left many warm friends there, among whom were the Rev. Abiel Holmes, Professor Willard and gentlemen connected with the College, and others. Very few of them were surviving twenty years later.

The purchase of the lands in Genessee County drew my father very much in his later years to Western New York. The investment was advantageous, but it was the occasion of immense trouble and anxiety, owing chiefly to the dishonesty of the agent whom he employed, and who had previously been acting for Mr. Craigie. This man was exceedingly artful and had completely deceived Mr. Craigie, and it was some time before his frauds were detected by my father. After being exposed and compelled to make restitution, so far as his embezzlements could be traced, he became my father's declared and unscrupulous enemy, and occasioned him very great difficulty and annoyance. My father was of a temperament sensitive and excitable, and these irritations disturbed greatly the repose of his declining years, and I have no doubt shortened his life.

In order to be near the scene of his business and give personal attention thereto my father purchased about the year 1821 the farm on the beautiful Skaneateles Lake, which he made subsequently his summer residence, and where he died. He had previously owned a considerable farm with a neat cottage on the Cayuga Lake, near the village of the same name. This he sold upon purchasing the Skaneateles place. The latter property is very finely situated, about two miles above the outlet, containing 250 acres, and bordering on the lake for a quarter of a mile. It was a residence in which your grandfather greatly delighted. He enjoyed his favorite pursuit of farming and constructed a boat in which he made frequent excursions on the Lake, and sounded its depths heretofore reported unfathomable. After his death this property was sold to Captain Nash DeCost of New York.

Although of robust frame and iron constitution, your grandfather's health, for a number of years before his death, was far from good. He felt the effects of the hardships and exposure of his earlier life. He suffered from sharp attacks of gout and rheumatism, and a severe influenza in the winter of 1825 gave a shock to his system from which he never fully recovered. In August, 1828, he was seized with what proved to be his last illness, of a dropsical nature. None of his family were with him at the time. Letters were then three or four days on the way from Skaneateles to Norwich, and the journey took as long a time. Immediately upon hearing of his alarming illness I started from Norwich, but only arrived after he had been more than twenty-four hours dead. The funeral had been appointed for the same afternoon, the warm weather forbidding longer delay. There was a very large gathering of friends and neighbours, and directions left by himself in a letter addressed to S. P. Horton, Esq., were carried out. The service of the Episcopal Church was

Extracts from a letter to his wife, written in 1823.

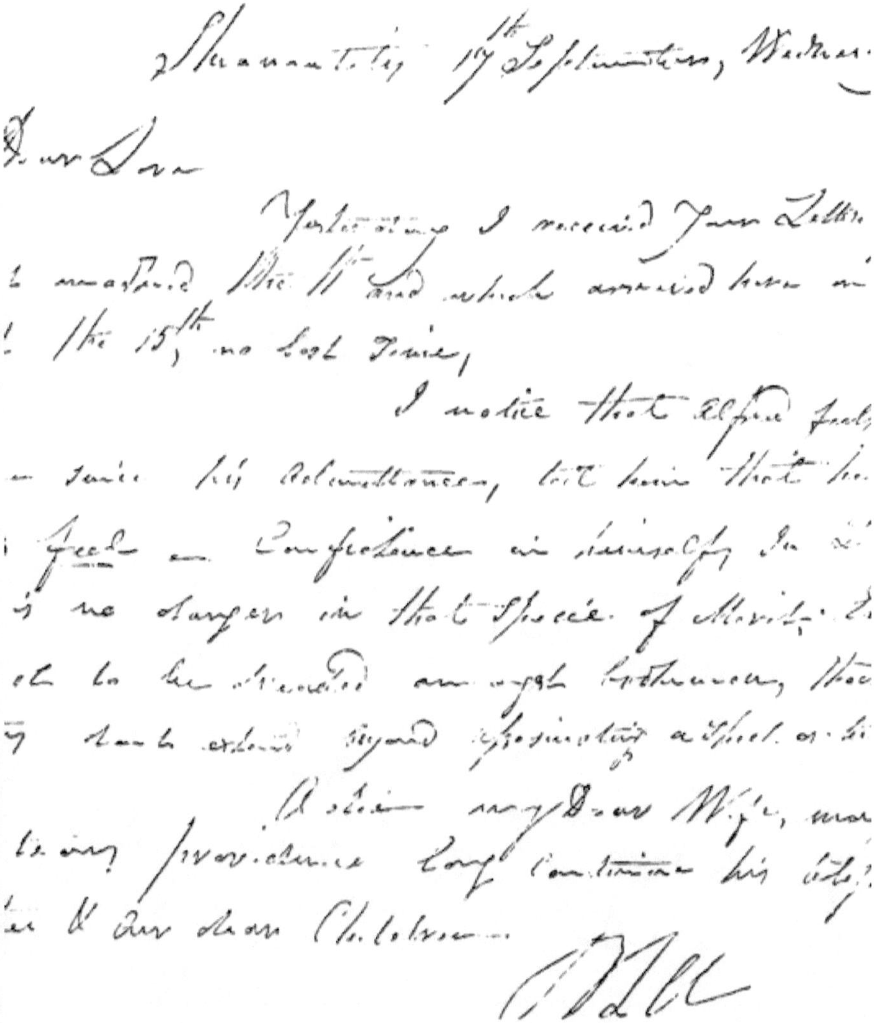

[illegible] 17th September, Wednes[illegible]

Dear [illegible]

Yesterday I received Your Letter [illegible] marked the 11th and which arrived here on the 15th, in Good Time,

I notice that Alfred feels [illegible] since his Admittance, tell him that he [illegible] feel [illegible] Confidence in himself, for there is no danger in that Species of Merit [illegible] to be blended amongst Bashfulness, [illegible]

Adieu my Dear Wife, may [illegible] Providence long continue his [illegible] [illegible] & our dear Children

[illegible]

read by the Rev. Mr. Hollister—the coffin was placed on the wheels of his open carriage and drawn by his own black horses, and his remains were deposited in a place chosen by himself not far from the dwelling house. This piece of ground was afterwards enclosed by a heavy stone wall, and was reserved when the farm was sold. The next spring a white marble obelisk was placed over the grave, inscribed with his name and dates of birth and death. The latter date was August 15, 1828. The general manifestations of sorrow and regret testified the high estimation in which he was held. No one of the family but myself was present at the funeral, my mother and Thomas arriving the next day.

Of late years the massive stone wall had begun to crack and bulge. It became evident that when no one of the family could give personal care and attention to the burial place, it would at length fall into ruins and the grave be left exposed. A beautiful rural cemetery had been laid out not far from the village, the Lake View Cemetery, and the choice of an eligible lot was offered to me on the part of the directors by E. N. Leslie, Esq. The regulations of this Cemetery provide for keeping it in good order by the income from sale of lots. It seemed to me that the expressed wishes of my father for a peaceful resting place would be best effected by the transfer thither of his remains. Accordingly, after consulting several members of the family, I took measures for this purpose and had the transfer made under my own eye on the 23d September, 1874, being very kindly assisted by Mr. Leslie in the performance of this mournful duty. The monument had been previously removed and placed beside the grave. There is from this point a most delightful prospect of the lake and village, and there is no fear of any future desecration. As I saw for the second time my father's grave filled up, and looked over the enchanting landscape as the declining sun threw his soft mellow light over the scene, every thing breathing peace and repose, I felt assured that all was arranged just as he himself would have desired.

I here insert two just and appropriate tributes to his memory. The first, supposed to be from the pen of his neighbour, William P. Greene, Esq., appeared in the Norwich Courier.

"At Skaneateles, N. Y., on the 15th instant, Benjamin Lee, Esq., of this City. Few deaths would excite more public sympathy. Mr. Lee had been absent from his family several months, residing at his seat in Skaneateles to superintend his property in the State of New York, where he was attacked with a disease of the chest which made such rapid progress that his family did not arrive in time to take a final leave of him. As a gentleman he was possessed of great urbanity—as a man, in all his business transactions upright, generous and high minded—to those who needed aid and whom he considered deserving, his charities were liberal and unostentatious. Benevolence was the prominent trait of his character, and no individual is probably left among us whose death will be more sensibly felt by the deserving poor. Justice demands this tribute of grateful respect to his memory. The private and unobtrusive manner in which the deceased chose to distribute his charities forbids that more should be said. Time may reveal the unknown author of many acts of beneficence."

The second notice appeared at Auburn, N. Y., and was probably written by the Hon. Daniel Kellogg.

"Died on the 15th August, instant, at his summer residence in Skaneateles, Benjamin Lee, Esq., of Norwich, Conn., in the 64th year of his age. His friends have lost a companion endeared to them by his kind and generous nature no less than by his rich and highly cultivated understanding, and his immediate relatives who felt and knew his worth and goodness, will find a void in their social circle which can never be supplied. Eminently distinguished for kindness and warm affection for his family, he deservedly enjoyed their love and veneration, and their deep sorrow in this bereavement is somewhat alleviated by the sympathy of the community. His condescension and the open-handed munificence with which he administered to the wants and necessities of the poor around him, can never be forgotten by any who have been guided and consoled by his affectionate counsel, or cherished and relieved by his unbounded charity."

In person your grandfather was a man to attract notice. He was six feet in height, but so erect in carriage and well developed that he was commonly supposed to be still taller. Those of the family who strike me as most nearly resembling him in countenance were his daughter Elizabeth and her daughter Ellen Dwight. Compact and muscular he possessed in his prime unusual physical strength and vigor, and to the last he was little susceptible to the influence of cold. His hair turned gray very early, and I remember his wearing it powdered and tied in a cue. His first appearance in pantaloons made quite an impression on his children, who had been accustomed to see him in small clothes with high boots and gold knee buckles. His manners were those of the gentleman of the old school, polite and urbane. In his family he was very kindly and affectionate, but accustomed for so many years to absolute authority on board ship he required prompt obedience and could not brook contradiction. He had the Englishman's partiality for horses and dogs. He usually had three or four horses in his stable, fine animals, and his daily recreation was a drive, often with an open carriage and pair. The dogs were always eager to accompany him, and indicating their delight with loud barking, the start of the carriage was often attended with a commotion quite exciting and gratifying to our childish ears. Sometimes the dogs were shut up to avoid this uproar, but soon getting to understand this, they would hide themselves before the customary hour, and when the equipage was fairly on the road would come bounding over the fences with noisy delight. My father made his frequent long journeys with his own horses. For these journeys considerable preparation was made. He usually took with him a bottle of essence of coffee, made under his own direction, so that he might not be dependent for that beverage upon country taverns, and some packages of hard gingerbread. He started by daylight and made nearly one-half of the days' journey before breakfast, averaging about forty or fifty miles per day. On these journeys I was often his companion, and have not forgotten how during the long cold morning drive, I enjoyed the gingerbread. So different was the estimate then of our territory that he commonly spoke of his journey to the Genessee region as going to the "Western Country." Highwaymen were not unknown, and his loaded pistols were fitted into the carriage seat by his side.

The religious preferences of your grandfather, as has been already mentioned, were in favor of the Episcopal Church. While we resided in Cambridge the church there was seldom supplied with regular ministrations, and my father's personal regard for Dr. Holmes led to the attendance of the family in the pew belonging to his brother in the old Congregational Church. On removing to Norwich he gave his support to the Episcopal Church, although, being troubled with vertigo in a close or crowded room, he seldom attended public worship. To the Church and Sunday School at Skaneateles he was a liberal contributor, and to this day the interest of a donation made by him is appropriated to the Sunday School Library. He often spoke of the goodness and greatness of God, and particularly enjoyed reading the Psalms. I remember his relating a dream which indicated that his mind was often occupied with meditation upon divine things. He was conversing, he thought, with Mr. Harrison Gray Otis (an eminent lawyer of Boston) and said to him, "Mr. Otis have you ever met with a composition to be compared with the Lord's Prayer?"

I believe that all the material facts within my recollection have been embraced within this sketch, and I am sure you will agree with me that the subject of it is a man to be remembered and held in honor by his descendants. May the good name, better than riches, which they inherit from him never be dimmed or tarnished by those in whose veins his blood shall run.

Your grandmother as you know survived her husband nearly forty-three years. Her benignant countenance, delightful home and green old age are fresh in your memories. On the 3d day of May, 1871, having nearly completed ninety-five years, at Norwich, Connecticut, she fell asleep in Jesus, her one surviving child and numerous loving grandchildren rising up to call her blessed.

J. B. LIPPINCOTT & CO.

Family Record

Benjamin Lee, born at Taunton, Somersetshire, England, Feby 26th 1765.
Died at Skaneateles, New York, August 15th 1828.

Elizabeth, daughter of John and Elizabeth Gorham Leighton born at Lunenburg, Massachusetts, Septr 22nd 1776.
Died at Norwich, Connecticut, May 3rd 1871.

BENJAMIN LEE and ELIZABETH LEIGHTON were married in the city of Boston, May 27th 1797, Rev. Dr. Belknap officiating.

Descendants

OF

Benjamin and Elizabeth Lee.

Children of Benjamin and Elizabeth Lee.

THOMAS, born at Medford, Massachusetts, March 21, 1798; died at Burlington, New Jersey, April 16, 1866.

ELIZABETH, born at Lancaster, Massachusetts, August 16, 1801; died at Springfield, Massachusetts, January 8, 1865.

PITT, born at Lancaster, Massachusetts, July 28, 1804; died August 6, 1804.

MARY, born at Cambridge, Massachusetts, December 15, 1805; died at Huntingdon, Pennsylvania, October 26, 1839.

ALFRED, born at Cambridge, Massachusetts, September 9, 1807.

BENJAMIN, born at Cambridge, Massachusetts, July 14, 1809; died August 16, 1809.

EDMUND, born at Cambridge, Massachusetts, July 16, 1810; died at Peperill, Massachusetts, August 11, 1836.

EMILY, born at Cambridge, Massachusetts, November 17, 1813; died in the city of New York, March 9, 1864.

CONSTANTINE, born at Cambridge, Massachusetts, January 23, 1819; died January 26, 1819.

Thomas Lee.

THOMAS LEE, born at Medford, Massachusetts, March 21, 1798; died at Burlington, New Jersey, April 16, 1866.

MARY REBECCA BOYCE, born at Havre de Grace, Maryland, October 9, 1803; died in the city of Philadelphia, April 21, 1871.

Thomas Lee and Mary Rebecca Boyce were married in St. Paul's Church, city of Philadelphia, by the Rev. Benjamin Allen, October 18, 1825.

Children of Thomas and Mary R. Lee.

MARY, born at Roxborough, Philadelphia, August 31, 1829; Married to Marshall S. Shapleigh, May 28, 1867.

ELIZABETH LEIGHTON, born at Philadelphia, August 28, 1831; died in the city of New York, January 11, 1837.

JANE BOYCE, born at New York, August 12, 1834. Married to Alexander Frederick Sabine, May 9, 1872.

CHARLES CHAUNCEY, born at Philadelphia, June 2, 1838; died September 9, 1839.

THOMAS, born at Philadelphia, September 10, 1842. Married to Caroline Morrell, March 5, 1874.

Elizabeth Lee.

ELIZABETH LEE, born at Lancaster, Massachusetts, August 16, 1801; died at Springfield, Massachusetts, January 8, 1865.

JAMES SANFORD DWIGHT, born at Springfield, Massachusetts, December 10, 1799; died at Florence, Italy, February 24, 1831.

James Sanford Dwight and Elizabeth Lee were married in Norwich, Connecticut, September 3, 1823, by the Rev. S. B. Paddock.

Elizabeth Dwight was married to John Turvil Adams, September 7, 1839.

Children of James S. and Elizabeth Dwight.

ELIZABETH LEE, born at Springfield, Massachusetts, July 27, 1824. Married to Fordyce Barker, M.D., September 14, 1843.

MARY SANFORD, born at Springfield, Massachusetts, October 13, 1826. Married to David Ames Wells, May 9, 1860.

ELLEN AUGUSTA, born at Springfield, Massachusetts, July 23, 1829.

Mary Lee.

MARY LEE, born at Cambridge, Massachusetts, December 5, 1805; died at Huntingdon, Pennsylvania, October 26, 1839.

WILLIAM HENRY, son of Lyman and Elizabeth Learned Law, born at New London, Connecticut, September 11, 1803.

William Henry Law and Mary Lee were married at Norwich, Connecticut, February 17, 1829, by the Rev. S. B. Paddock.

ELIZABETH LEIGHTON, only child of William Henry and Mary Law, born at Norwich, Connecticut, November 7, 1829. Married to the Rev. Treadwell Walden, September 15, 1858.

Alfred Lee.

ALFRED LEE, born at Cambridge, Massachusetts, September 9, 1807.

JULIA, daughter of Elihu and Sarah Trumbull White, born at Hartford, Connecticut, September 21, 1811.

Alfred Lee and Julia White were married in Grace Church, City of New York, April 23, 1832, by the Rev. J. M. Wainwright.

Children of Alfred and Julia White Lee.

BENJAMIN, born at Norwich, Connecticut, September 26, 1833. Married to Emma Hale White, April 5, 1859.

LEIGHTON, born at Norwich, Connecticut, September 20, 1837; died in Philadelphia, February 13, 1853.

MARY, born at Wilmington, Delaware, April 17, 1842; died in Wilmington, April 26, 1842.

CLEMENTINA SMITH, born at Wilmington, Delaware, April 10, 1846. Married to Rev. Charles E. McIlvaine, November 14, 1867.

ELIZABETH LEIGHTON and JULIA TRUMBULL, twin daughters, born at Wilmington, Delaware, April 8, 1849. Elizabeth Leighton, died at Wilmington, November 12, 1850. Julia Trumbull, died at Philadelphia, November 4, 1870.

ALFRED, born at Wilmington, Delaware, March 25, 1852.

EDMUND, born at Wilmington, Delaware, March 9, 1855; died at Wilmington, Delaware, December 9, 1857.

Emily Lee.

EMILY LEE, born at Cambridge, Massachusetts, November 17, 1813; died in the City of New York, March 9, 1864.

DANIEL TYLER, son of Daniel and Sarah Edwards Tyler, born in Brooklyn, Connecticut, January 8, 1799.

Daniel Tyler and Emily Lee were married in Norwich, Connecticut, May 20, 1832, by the Rev. S. B. Paddock.

Children of Daniel and Emily Tyler.

ALFRED LEE, born at Norwich, Connecticut, May 19, 1834. Married to Annie E. Scott, in Macon, Georgia, May 25, 1859.

GERTRUDE ELIZABETH, born at Harrandsville, Pennsylvania, February 16, 1836. Married to Charles Carow, in Norwich, Connecticut, June 8, 1859.

EDMUND LEIGHTON, born at Harrandsville, Pennsylvania, May 2, 1838.

MARY LAW, born at Norwich, Connecticut, March 2, 1840. Married to Alexander Moore, U. S. A., April 1, 1875.

AUGUSTUS CLEVELAND, born at Norwich, Connecticut, May 2, 1851.

Family Record.

Family Record.

Family Record.

Family Record.

Family Record.

Family Record.

Family Record.

Family Record.

www.ingramcontent.com/pod-product-compliance
Lightning Source LLC
Chambersburg PA
CBHW020038030726
47499CB00007B/2491
9783337219826